W9-BLP-713

≠
E
C319g

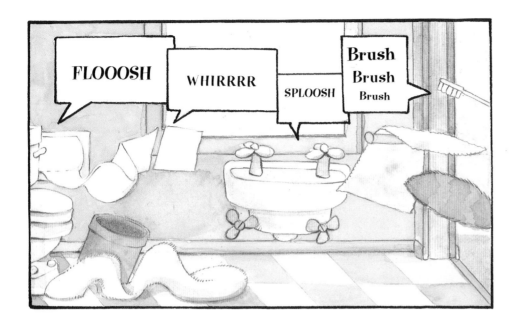

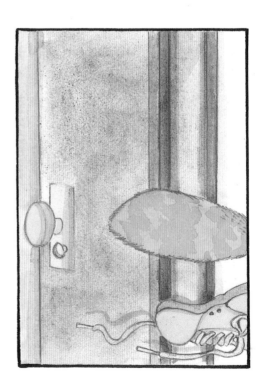

Good Morning, Maxine!

Story and pictures by Denys Cazet

Bradbury Press · New York

For Craig and Carolyn Bond
and, of course, Angie, Melissa, and Carly

Bradbury Press
An Affiliate of Macmillan, Inc.
866 Third Avenue, New York, NY 10022
Collier Macmillan Canada, Inc.
Printed and bound in Japan
First American Edition
10 9 8 7 6 5 4 3 2 1

The text is set in Pixie. The illustrations are rendered in
pen-and-ink and watercolor.

LIBRARY OF CONGRESS CATALOGING-IN-PUBLICATION DATA
Cazet, Denys.
   Good morning, Maxine!/by Denys Cazet.
      p.   cm.
   Summary: Maxine is told to go straight to school, a
directive it is really impossible for that irrepressible,
adventuresome cat to fulfill.
   ISBN 0-02-717940-0
   [1. Cats—Fiction.]   I. Title.
PZ7.C2985Go   1989   [E]—dc 19
88-2889   CIP   AC

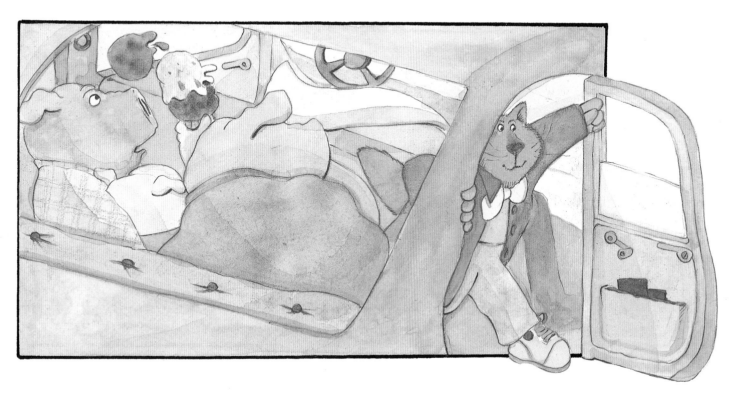

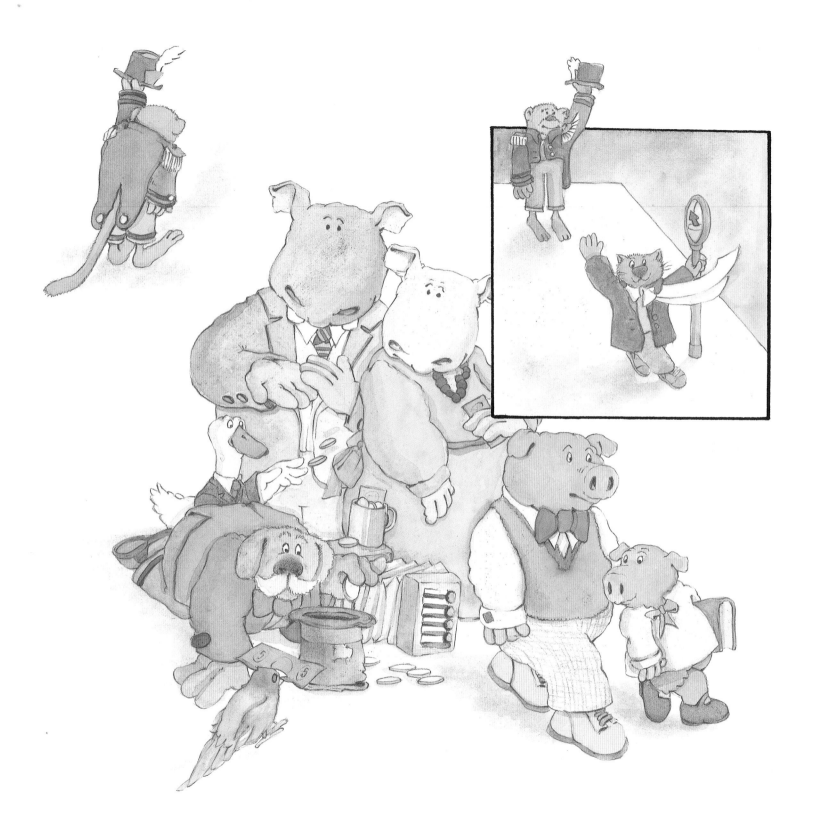

THUNK!

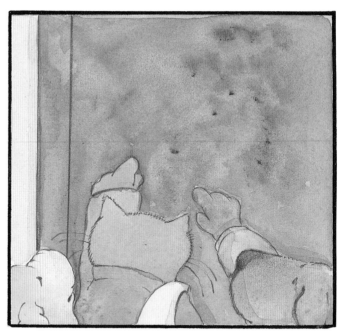

Well? Go on...
straight to room four.

Straight as
an arrow?

Yes, Maxine!
STRAIGHT AS AN ARROW.

OK. But,
you better
hold this,
Mr. Potts.